FROM SEA TO SHINING SEA

Joyce MacBeth Morehouse
FROM SEA TO SHINING SEA

Published by BooxAi
ISBN: 978-965-577-971-4

FROM SEA TO SHINING SEA

JOYCE MACBETH MOREHOUSE

Contents

Chapter 1

"I really enjoy weekends. I like having them off so we can do as we please."

"I must say, I agree with you 100%. It's so nice to get up when we want and enjoy a leisurely breakfast. Maybe I do drink too much coffee on weekends, but it's so relaxing to have nothing in particular to do. Perhaps we should take a walk down the path behind the house. We've never gone down there since we moved here. It's time we explored the place a bit more, don't you think?"

"Owen, I can hardly believe you're suggesting a walk. The only walking I've ever known you to do is at the golf course. I think I'm becoming a golf widow."

"Oh, come on, Kim, be fair! You used to go golfing with me."

"Yes, it was something to do while I waited to be a mother,

but since Dr. Socoe filled us in on the details yesterday, I know that I'll most likely never have a child of my own. You might as well know...I'd like to adopt. How do you feel about that?"

"Uh, uh, I'm not so sure. Do you think that would make you happy?

"Absolutely, Owen. But I also want to adopt a helpless little Orphan from a Foreign Country where they don't stand a chance. Seeing that more than five years worth of attempts have failed, I agree adopting is the way to go. Furthermore, Dr.Socoe suggested that there are many orphans in Asian countries waiting for adoption."

"Are you sure that's where you want to go for a child?"

"Of course! They have plenty to pick from and so many are anxious to have parents."

"I'll tell you what! We'll make a deal. If we can find what we want in China, we'll bring her home with us."

Kim leaped up off her chair and went to sit on her husband's knee. Putting her arm about his neck, she whispered, "I love you, Owen."

As she sat facing the window, she saw a stranger on the highway walking past their house, but he stopped and stared up the driveway for several minutes before moving on. He must have gone only a short distance before turning around and walking back.

"Don't move, Owen, or he'll see you, but look ahead and you'll see a rather strange man stopping in front of our driveway. He keeps looking up here, but I'm not sure why. If we sit very still, he may not notice us and will go away."

"Uh oh! I think he just saw us. Now he's coming in the driveway. What do you suppose he wants?"

They sat very still, thinking perhaps he hadn't noticed them and watched him approach. He would stop every once in awhile and gaze at the house, but it looked like he was proceeding to their back door.

Kim got up and sat on the sofa while they waited for his knock. After several minutes, Owen got up and went to the kitchen. There was no one there.

"I'm afraid he's disappeared on us, Kim."

"He couldn't just disappear! He must be out there somewhere in the backyard."

She came out and stepped outside with him. There was no one in sight.

"He couldn't have just disappeared. He has to be somewhere around!"

Suddenly, they both thought the same thing at the same time. The road in the woods.

As they glanced toward it, there was no one in sight. But there was nowhere else he could go.

"I'm more convinced than ever that we need to see where that walk through the woods leads."

"Owen, my love, I'm more anxious for you to arrange things with your boss, so we can head to China."

They continued to look around the property, then went back inside.

But where could that strange little man have gone?

Chapter 2

For the next few months, Owen made inquiries and they prepared for their trip to China. There were needles and medical appointments along with oodles of paperwork. Owen's boss granted him a six-month leave of absence.

As the day approached, Kim wondered if they were doing the right thing, but her husband felt this was the way to go.

Eight months later they found themselves landing on China's soil, where they were again faced with interrogation and uncertainty. Time passed swiftly and with more forms to fill out, they were busy until taken to the orphanage. They were overwhelmed by the number of children they encountered. Most were shy and avoided them, but one beautiful little girl soon captured their hearts. She was about a year and a half old. She came up to them, extended her arms and smiled. That was all it took and they made their decision. However, there was much more work to be done before they could take her with them. Her name was Chun Lee, but they decided to call her Astrid.

Finally, the day arrived and they hailed a taxi to take them to the airport. The journey was uneventful and they were soon entering their own home. Astrid was a bit strange as there were so many new things for her to see.

When their friends and neighbours heard about their arrival, they got together to welcome the little girl. In the presence of so many adults, Astrid grew hesitant and a bit shy.

"Oh! She's beautiful!" Their next-door neighbour exclaimed. She extended her arms to the little girl who went and stood behind a chair.

"I'm afraid she's not used to seeing so many adults surrounding her," Kim laughed.

Kim got out some cookies and made everyone a cup of tea while they chatted, then opened the many gifts they had brought for the child.

"Astrid, come see what you have here," Kim instructed, holding up a dress. The child failed to respond. It was obvious she was unfamiliar with the language. They hoped she would soon understand.

By 8 o'clock, the child was tired and Kim got her in her pyjamas as people began to disperse.

"Thank you so much for this nice surprise for our new daughter and please come again."

Owen saw the last person out. He was a friend of a neighbour, but new to their village.

"Thank you for coming and being a part of our neighbourhood."

The man tipped his hat and went off into the night.

"Well, that's over."

"Yes, and it was very nice of them. I'm going to take Astrid up to bed now. I'll be back in a few minutes! That is, if she settles down okay."

'What a beautiful summer evening,' Kim thought as she put the child in bed. She showed her how to fold her hands to pray, then said the childhood prayer, "Now I lay me down to sleep." As she finished, she noticed the child's questioning eyes looking at her.

"You'll soon get used to it and before you know it, you will be saying English words."

Kim tucked her in and went to the window to view the gorgeous sunset. To her amazement, the strange new neighbour, whom Owen had seen out, was standing just a short way from the window, looking up at the room. She knew that a trellis of roses climbed the wall just outside the window, and suddenly, Kim's stomach felt very queasy. What was that guy gazing up there for?

When the man noticed Kim looking out the window, he slowly turned and walked away.

Immediately, Kim moved the baby's crib across the hall to the room next to them. She hated moving her out of the room they had so beautifully decorated for the child, but 'better safe than sorry' was her next thought. She stayed with the little girl longer than she intended, but when she explained to Owen about the stranger, he too was concerned.

"You know," he said, "I didn't even hear the man's name."

"Neither did I! I'm not sure anyone told us his name. They just said he had recently moved into the local neighbourhood. But I find it just a bit scary the way he hung around until last and then stood watching outside."

"I guess there is no law to stop a man from looking around. I just wonder how close he lives to us."

"Maybe you could ask around tomorrow, Owen, and find out a few facts about him."

"Yes, I believe I will!"

Chapter 3

The next day dawned bright and beautiful and since Owen still had a month left in his leave of absence, he decided to use the day to get acquainted with his new neighbour and maybe glean some facts about him. He casually walked to the other end of the village where the Smiths lived. Ned Smith had said the stranger had moved In next to him, but Ned never told them his name. He would stop in to see Ned first and do some enquiring. He was almost sure to be home as he was retired. As he went in the driveway, Ned came out the door.

"Why, good morning neighbor," Ned called with a wave.

"Howdy, Friend! We've had a wonderful season this year. It sure is a gorgeous morning!"

"It is indeed. And what brings you here this fine day?"

"Just curiosity, I guess. You said you had a new neighbour move in. How far away is his place? I don't see his house."

"Oh! Right. You can't see the house from here. It's that old rundown farmhouse that's been vacant for years. I think he might be planning to fix it up a bit. If you go down around that curve in the road and glance back towards the woods, you'll recognize it. I should think it's almost opposite your house if you go back through that group of trees, seeing that this country road is almost horseshoe-shaped."

"Well, yes, it is, and I do believe you're right. We're probably closer neighbours if we go through the woods than if we walk the length of the village road."

"Are you planning to call on him? If so, I'd like to come with you."

"Sure enough! That's a great idea. What's his name, by the way?"

Ned looked at him curiously. "You know, Friend, I hate to admit it, but I really don't know. I don't believe he ever told us. We went over to invite him to the party we had at your house. He was in the yard, so we welcomed him as our new neighbour. My wife explained to him what was taking place at your house and I said he could go along with us if he liked. I'm not even sure he spoke, but he nodded assent to our invitation. He was fixing something on the gate entrance and he just kept on with his task."

"We'll see you tonight about 7:00 then."

"He nodded again and we took our leave. We did mention that we weren't sure it was a great idea as we had no clue where he came from. But we did think perhaps he was just a very introverted man who had come to this country village to be alone. I was slightly taken aback when we went out at 7:00 to get in the car and he was standing patiently beside it. I mentioned the fact that it was nice of him to come and meet some village folks, but he still didn't speak. Would it be possible that he can't speak, I wonder?"

"Most likely just a bit reticent. We'll soon know."

The two men had gone around the curve in the road so that the house was clearly visible. There was no one outside, so they walked up the rutted driveway to the old house. Ned knocked on the door, but there was no answer. They tried again and then decided that he had perhaps gone for a walk; maybe even to the little corner store, although he would have to pass Ned's house, and they hadn't seen him go by.

"Well, I must admit he could have passed easily as we don't make it a habit to watch for passers-by."

The men turned back toward Ned's. As they got near the driveway, Ned invited, "Why not come in for a visit and a cup of coffee? We don't get together that much."

"Don't mind if I do! The wife doesn't expect me home til lunch."

The two men went up the steps and entered the back door, but they stopped instantly as they heard voices from the doorway

"I'm sorry, but I can't invite you in as my husband isn't home. Since I am alone, it wouldn't be proper!"

"Surely you wouldn't deny a stranger a bite to eat. I'm mighty hungry and I AM your next door neighbour."

"Well, if you'll sit down on the step, I'll bring you some toast and coffee."

The two men heard her close the door, so they confronted her.

"Oh, Ned," she said, as she popped some bread in the toaster, " It's that man from next door and he was determined to come in!"

"It okay, Hun. I'll deal with it."

Owen and Ned made their way to the front door. His wife had locked it, but he quickly unlocked it and gasped in surprise. The stranger was not there!

"Where could he go so fast? Owen asked in surprise.

Chapter 4

Owen hadn't noticed that the sides of the 4 steps had been boarded in on each side all the way to the ground and Ned had forgotten about it. The stranger had simply slipped between the steps and sat quietly in the sheltered alcove.

When the two men had gone back to the kitchen and closed the front door, Ned told Nell the man was no longer around.

"He disappeared in thin air...no sign of him anywhere. I don't know how he does it, but I will say, he's pretty slick at it. We're looking for a cup of coffee and one of your doughnuts, Nell. How about that?"

"Would one of you like the slice of toast I got the stranger?"

"How about you?" Ned asked Owen.

"No, thanks, but I could eat a doughnut."

"Coming right up," Nell said as she brought them doughnuts and coffee. Ned decided he could also eat the toast.

"Any jam for this toast?"

"Just don't ruin your lunch!" Nell added, passing him the jam.

The men sat and talked, mostly about the stranger.

"You know, that man lives right opposite your place since this village road is shaped like a horseshoe. If you went straight back through the woods behind your house, you would come out just behind his house, I figure."

"You know, you're probably right! My house is on one end of the horseshoe and his would be on the other, so I guess we're not that far apart. Someday, I think I'll take a walk back through the woods and see where I come out...no doubt very near his place."

"I think before I go home to lunch, I'll take a walk back toward his place and see if he's home yet."

Owen got up from the table and thanked the hostess as he made his way to the door.

"Hold it! I'm coming with you." Ned got up and the two of them went out. The stranger's house was not visible from their place, but as soon as they rounded the curve in the road, they saw the ramshackle old farmhouse. It sat back almost to the woods.

"Wow. It really does need lots of work. I hope he's a good worker."

"It needs a new roof for sure. I wonder if he'll ask anyone to help."

"That's pretty hard to say, but I promise you, I wouldn't go up on that roof for anything!" Ned said, "I'm not only too old, but I'm mighty chicken too. I wouldn't touch it. But then again, he's not a very friendly fellow, so he might prefer to work alone."

As they walked toward the house, there didn't seem to be anyone around. Ned knocked on the door and when there was no answer, he tried again, but without results. They turned and went back up the road toward Neds, where they parted ways, Owen heading on home.

"Hi! I made it home before lunch just like you told me to."

"I'm afraid lunch isn't quite ready. I've been playing with Astrid, but now you can take over and I'll get lunch on. What did you find out about the stranger?"

"Nothing I didn't already know...that he's a stranger without a name."

Kim took a potato scallop from the oven and brought out some warm biscuits, filled their glasses with water and cut some cheese. She made mention that the scallop was one of Owen's favourites as she had chopped up some ham in it.

"Sounds mighty good to me!"

"I'll put Astrid in her highchair, but you can get started if you like."

"No hurry here. I'll wait for you and Astrid." He didn't tell her that he had eaten a doughnut about an hour earlier.

Kim put Astrid in her chair and cut up some grapes and peaches for her, then added some bites of cheese, some crackers and a glass of milk. As she sat down, Owen reached over and took the baby's hand. Kim reached for his other hand while he said grace. As they ate, Owen related the story of the stranger's disappearance at Neds.

"Owen Boone! Have you been drinking?"

"Woman, you know very well that I don't drink. Haven't touched it in years...not since I came to the Lord years ago! You know that!"

"Sounds to me like you both had a nip. How does a man just disappear?"

"You know Ned doesn't touch it either. We're both on the church board. I can't believe you would say such a thing!"

"I just can't imagine you were both in your right minds. That man is a puzzle for sure."

Owen turned to the baby. " Are you doing any talking, Astrid?" He inquired. "Can you say 'dada' yet? Come on say, 'dada' 'dada'."

Astrid looked at him, held up a piece of cheese and said some foreign word.

"I wonder if you'll ever speak English."

"I think she will in time. I've been trying to get her to understand some of our terms. I dropped a piece of paper on the floor the other day and said, 'pick it up'. She just stared at me, even though I did it over and over. Yesterday, I thought I would try one more time, so I threw down the paper. Before I had a chance to say a word, she said, 'pit it up'. When I did, she giggled hysterically, so I'm sure it's just a matter of time before she will be using English words."

"You could be right," Owen answered as he got up from the table and Kim took Astrid from the high chair.

"I'm going to put her down for an afternoon nap. Before I do, is there anything special you'd like for supper?"

"Whatever you want to get. Meanwhile, I'm going to take a stroll into town this afternoon. Is there anything you would like me to get while I'm there?"

"I can't think of anything. Have a pleasant walk."

Owen kissed his wife on the forehead as she went past him toward the stairs. He waved at his daughter and repeated his 'bye bye,' hoping she would learn to say the same. As he left the house, he actually thought of taking the car, then realized it was too dirty to be seen in public, so he stopped long enough to get the hose and give it a good spray-down. He decided he probably should walk, after all, so went toward their 'shopping centre' in the town area.

Kim put Astrid down for her afternoon nap and took a look out the window. To her horror, the stranger was stopped on the highway, glaring up at the window. He must have noticed her putting the baby to bed. She quickly retreated out of his sight but watched from a distance as he began his awkward stroll once again. She stayed in the room for quite some time, hoping that was the end of him.

Once in town, Owen went straight to the police station. He knew everyone there and they knew him, so he decided to ask for their help in identifying the stranger.

"Well, well! We haven't seen you in awhile!"

"You're absolutely right, Sergeant! We were away for

awhile too. I had a six-month leave from my job and went to China."

"So I hear. And you came home with a baby girl. Congratulations!"

"Thank you! We do have a lovely little Chinese girl. But that's not my problem today. I'm here to inquire about a recent neighbour whose activities leave something to be desired."

"And what's his name?"

"That's part of the problem. Nobody knows."

"Hmmm ...that is rather unusual, but we don't normally investigate unless he has wronged someone."

Owen tried giving him a brief description of the man.

"Well, I guess it wouldn't hurt to take a ride out there. Besides, it's always nice to make the acquaintance of someone new to our village."

"Would it be possible for me to ride along?"

"Uhhh....I suppose that would be alright, seeing as how you know exactly where he lives."

The two men got in the police car and headed out of the town area.

Chapter 5

"About a mile beyond my place is the Smith house. You know who I'm speaking of, don't you? Ned Smith, who is on the Life Church Board with me, lives next to the old house the stranger is occupying. Possibly you know where Ned lives."

"Yes, I think I do. Everyone in the village knows Ned. I've been to his place once before when someone stole his plow. Thank goodness, we were able to track that down."

"Then let's hope you can do the same this time! We need to know a little more about our new neighbour. We wouldn't be so worried if his actions were more normal, but I have a basic mistrust of anyone who doesn't disclose his name and behaves in the manner he's been behaving. I'm not quite sure I trust the man."

"Well, I'm quite sure we'll soon find out who he is."

As the two approached and rounded the curve, the

policeman said, "Yes, I see the old house, but I don't think I've ever noticed it before. It's a pretty abandoned-looking place alright! Why would he want that old house?"

As they turned into the driveway, Owen caught sight of the stranger hurrying into the woods behind the house.

"There he goes! He's gone into the woods back there! Did you see that?"

"I'm afraid I didn't."

The policeman sighed in frustration. "How did I miss that? Shall we go into the woods after him?"

"That's up to you, but you know we might just catch up with him when he comes out on the other end, near the town, if you think we should drive back there - or, you can always try chasing him through the woods."

"Then let's go back to town and wait for him to exit."

They turned back out on the road and proceeded in the direction from which they had just come. There were two or three exits from the woods into the town area, but they chose the one which they thought was most likely to be from the Boone place. The Sergeant first checked in at the office, where all seemed well.

"No excitement here today, Constable?" He asked the Cop on duty.

"No, Sir. Nothing so far."

"I'm going out again. We may have something in the near future. I'll let you know later."

Once back in the car, Owen and the policeman sat

watching and waiting. In fact, they waited until the policeman chose to leave.

"I'll get my other two men working on this in the next few days. I agree there's something fishy going on here, but I'm not sure what it is. We need to first identify the man. Then we can put some tracers out on him. I have no idea why he disappears when he leaves the house, but we will get to the bottom of this!"

"Then I should get on home."

Owen started to open the car door.

"Wait! I'll drive you home."

"Thank you," Owen replied, "And we need to keep our eyes open. There are not too many hiding places for a man in this small village."

As they drew near the Boone home, Owen suddenly cried out, "There he is! He's standing right behind our house. But what is he looking at?"

The policeman jammed on his brakes and both men jumped out and started running toward the house. By the time they got in the backyard, the stranger was gone.

"Quick! Into the woods," Owen cried.

They tried to get sight of the man as they went down the path into the woods, but apparently, they could not overtake him. They walked back towards the house, talking about him as they went. They walked directly beside the tall tree in which he was hiding. Once they had gone out of sight, the stranger climbed down and headed for the lonely old house.

He hoped they didn't catch him before he had achieved his goal.

When Owen got home, Kim was crying and rocking their daughter.

"Oh, Owen, I thought you would never get back and that ugly stranger stood looking up at Astrid's room in the most frightening way. I finally just came down and decided to rock her awhile. I hope she doesn't sense my fear."

Owen pressed his wife's shoulder in a comforting manner. "Don't worry about it, Dear. The police are working on it. They'll keep an eye on things and eventually get him, I hope."

"Oh, that's such a relief! But until they find out what's going on, I'll be uneasy!

Owen said nothing aloud, but he was thinking, 'So will I!'

Chapter 6

Astrid was awake and crying. Kim hurried upstairs and picked her up. She changed her diaper and put her in the bath, where she splashed happily until Kim got her clean clothes together. She finished washing her, dried her off and took her down to her high chair. She gave her a cup of milk and a bowl of cereal, then

followed it with some goldfish crackers.

Owen came in from his morning walk and took his daughter out of her chair.

"Astrid wants to play ball with dada?"

"Bah," she said, reaching for the ball he was holding.

"Wow, Kim, did you hear that? She said ball."

Kim smiled. "I told you she would soon learn."

He took the child into the living room and got down on the floor with her, where they began rolling the ball.

Kim made fresh coffee and asked if he would like a cup. He put some other toys down for Astrid and went to join his wife at the table. For once, their talk did not centre on the stranger. They were engrossed in conversation when Kim suddenly exclaimed, "Don't move from where you are but take a look sideways at the west window. Isn't that the stranger coming up our driveway?"

Owen glanced sideways. "It certainly looks that way. Maybe he's coming in for a chat, though I doubt it. Do you think he can see us sitting here in the middle of the room?"

"I don't think so, not at this angle, but I do wish you would lock both doors. I don't want him just walking in. Stop and get the baby and bring her in here with us."

Owen got up and locked both doors, but when he picked up Astrid to take her to the kitchen, she started crying, wanting her toys. Owen reached for several of her toys. Meanwhile, Kim was watching the stranger approach the house. He would take a few steps, stop and look around, but when the baby started crying, he stopped and gazed at the upstairs windows. Kim moved to a safe distance so he could not see, but when she looked back out, he was gone. Where could he go so fast?

Owen came in and put the baby down with her toys, then glanced out the window.

"It's okay. He's gone."

"But gone where? I had my back turned for only a minute and he disappeared. Where could he go? He was almost up to the door the last time I saw him."

"He can be very stealthy. He sure knows how to make a quick escape! I'm going outside to look around."

The stranger quickly stepped to the back of the house. He heard the front door open and looked about. He didn't have time to reach the road to the woods without being caught. Speedily he plunged behind the climbing rose bush going up beside the bedroom window. He heard the steps coming around the house and did his best to hide himself in the climbing roses. He figured things were almost over for him. What could he do if he were discovered? He heard steps going up to the back door beside him. But they came down again and he heard them receding. He tried to get sight of whoever it was but heard the steps go off in the distance. Had they gone into the woods in search of him? If so! He needed to get out of here and back to the highway. He could lumber back to the house at leisure and no one would suspect anything. He waited a few minutes, then made his escape.

Kim watched him hurry out the driveway with his limping gait. He got on the road and started back toward his place, hurrying at first, then slowing down to a leisurely pace. She wished Owen would come back. He could possibly follow him and overtake him. Maybe he could even learn his name. In about twenty minutes, Owen came in. Sure enough, he had walked through the woods to the stranger's house but again, there was no one there. He even knocked at the door, but no one answered. When he tried to turn the knob, the door opened easily.

"Hello! Anyone here?"

Owen was tempted to step inside but figured that might not be the wise thing to do. He didn't want to be tried for 'break and enter,' but one could never tell what the strange old man might do.

Meanwhile, the stranger thought while travelling the highway, 'Why didn't I go up that climbing rose bush after he went into the woods? I could have been in the baby's room by now. I have to get hold of my contact tonight and he'll accuse me of missing my chance.'

As he came around the curve in the highway just before his place, he caught sight of someone just coming down the steps of the old house. He scurried back around the curve and stepped off the road to wait. After quite some time, he determined that whoever it was had gone back through the woods, so he made his way homeward once again very cautiously. There was no one in sight, so he went uneasily up the rutted driveway. He hadn't eaten yet today, so he put some water in the old coffee pot and looked around for some food. All he could find was a few crackers and some peanut butter. They would do.

Owen was back in under thirty minutes.

"I'm glad you're back. The police department called. You can call them back. Maybe they'll have some info on the stranger. I hope they found out who he was and what he's doing here."

Owen took the phone from his wife and dialled the number.

Chapter 7

Owen picked up the phone and dialled the Police Headquarters.

"Good Morning, Sergeant. This is Owen Boone and I believe you wanted to speak to me. Is now a good time?"

"I wanted to let you know that we're still trying to get the name of this fellow and we have several questionable characters show up on our search, but no one who looks like him. Do you suppose you could come in tomorrow morning and we'll let you look them over? You would know more about how he looks than we do. I can tell you one thing! There is no one here that you would WANT to see. Their records are terrible. But since this lad doesn't seem to be amongst them, he may not be so bad, after all."

"No problem, sir! I'll be there about 9 a.m., DV."

"And what does DV mean?"

"Uh, it's a term I use a lot, Sir...practically every day. It means 'Lord willing'"

"Then let's hope we catch this guy and that the Lord is willing."

"Okay, Sergeant! I'll hope to see you at 9 a.m. tomorrow."

Morning dawned with a constant drizzle.

"Oh! Oh! No going outside this morning, Astrid. I know how you like to play outside and if it had been a nice day, I would have taken you out to your swing for awhile, but unless it quickly clears up, we will stay indoors."

Kim kept Astrid busy with her toys until 10:30 a.m., when she put her down for her morning nap. She also noticed that the drizzle had turned to a mist and by the time Astrid got up from her nap, the sun had come out. By the time they finished lunch, things outside had dried off nicely and Astrid then kept running to the door, obviously wanting out. Kim took advantage of the situation to teach her the word 'out'. She kept asking, "'out?' Astrid...out?" After she repeated it a few times, the child caught on and said 'out'. Kim picked her up in a giant hug and they went down the back steps to the swing. Astrid loved her slide and her swing, so for awhile, they alternated between them. About 2 o'clock, the child began to be getting sleepy, so Kim took her to the big lawn chair and sat down with her. Astrid quickly climbed up and laid her head on Kim's shoulder, nodding off sleepily. Kim carefully rose from the chair, intending to carry the little girl to her crib! But as she did so, she caught a glimpse of movement in the woods. Her breath caught in her throat...what if she had left the child for a minute to use the bathroom or get the baby a drink? She felt faint and was seized with a sense of panic as she hurried up the steps to the back door, locking it behind her. In so doing, Astrid awoke and began to fuss. Kim hurriedly fixed her a bottle of milk and put her in her crib. In no time she had gone back to sleep, but Kim could not convince herself to go downstairs and leave the child alone.

Owen didn't get home until after 4 p.m., but by this time, Astrid and Kim were both downstairs. Kim was preparing supper and Astrid was following her around, wanting to help. Kim finally held her up and let her put the carrots and turnips in the stew. Kim added the doughboys after the vegetables were nearly done and she left a bit of dough on the counter for Astrid to play with. The child was easy to entertain and would keep herself busy with the dough.

Kim could barely contain herself when Owen came in.

"Well, did they catch him or find out who he is?"

"I'm afraid not. I went all through the pictures they pulled up in Search but didn't see the stranger. There was one blank space, though...there was only a description, no picture for it, but it was in their WANTED list."

"What did it say about the missing picture?"

"Supposedly, he had broken out of an insane asylum. They did say he was improving and might try to pass as 'normal'. They did know his name. It's Gus Griffin, but they have no official picture. However, their asylum artist will try to put together a sketch of him and publish it as soon as possible.

The only thing is, the artist had just seen the guy once, so let's hope he has a good memory!"

"It might have done more good for them to be out searching today. I saw the guy at the edge of the woods when Astrid and I were outdoors!"

"Why didn't you give the police a call?"

"You know how he disappears! He would have been gone by the time the police arrived."

"I suppose you're right. We'll just have to see how the sketch helps. The police intend to go out there about 6 o'clock tomorrow morning."

"I only hope they catch him soon. I can't take much more of this!" Kim went about setting the table.

Chapter 8

"I wonder if he has any contacts?" The Sergeant was curious. He and Constable Andrews were starting out early the next morning.

"I wouldn't have a clue, but I sure wouldn't doubt it either."

"You know," the constable added, " I think I have an idea of something that might work. Why don't I act as a contact to see if we can get him out of the house? We will need to leave the car this side of the curve in the highway so he won't see it, then I could go to his door and announce myself as his contact."

"I have a better idea," said the Sergeant. "Let me be the contact! I'll leave you in the car to watch if he tries to get away!"

"Uh! Uh! I don't think that would work. You spotted him

the other day and he might recognize you. I've never seen him, nor he me, so I should be the contact."

"Maybe you're right." The Sergeant added grudgingly.

Constable Andrews grabbed a green shawl from the back seat and drew it over his shoulders as a bit of a disguise.

They pulled up almost to the curve in the road and the constable got out.

"Let me know if you need help!"

"I will," Andrews answered as he went around the curve toward the house. In a few minutes, he had stationed himself just beside the door of the old house. He knocked loudly.

When there was no response, he called out as softly as he could (supposing he had awakened the stranger with his loud knock). "Your contact here!"

He listened as the old man shuffled toward the door

"Are you Alfred Snow?"

"I told you, I'm your contact. Do you have the child?"

"I can explain! Just a minute."

The constable supposed he was getting his clothes on and in a few minutes, the door opened slowly. Constable Andrews was on him immediately. He had him by the collar and pushed him ahead of him down the steps. "Away we go! Now, what is your name?"

"There was no answer from the stranger. He kept his head down and limped slowly along toward the police car. Andrews pushed him in the back seat and continued questioning him, only to no avail. He decided to try some special police tactics.

"Are you Gus Griffin?" No answer.

As they took him into the police precinct, the Sergeant took over the questioning. He also went back to the Search to see if he had a sketch yet. It was there but looked nothing like the stranger. The only recognizable feature was an old hat pulled down nearly over his eyes. Apparently, he had always worn a hat like that. They called Owen Boone to come in to see if he could recognize him.

It was 8:30 a.m. and Owen was having breakfast, but he took the call immediately.

"Yes, Sergeant, I'll be there shortly. I'm glad you caught him...at least, I'll know for sure when I see him."

Owen got up from the table, told his wife where he was going and hurried off.

"I'll be back about lunchtime! See you later." He gave his wife a peck on the cheek and hurried to his car.

At the police station, he was anxious to see the man. To his amazement, he looked totally different without his hat.

"There's something different about this guy, but I can't put my finger on it."

"Are you telling us you're not sure this is him? We need a positive identity!"

"Did they send you a sketch as promised?"

"Yes! We got a sketch but never having seen too much of him. It doesn't look like this guy."

"Could I see the sketch?"

"Oh, sure! Right this way."

The Sergeant went to Search and pulled up the sketch.

"There you go! Now does that look like him?"

Owen took one glance at the hat pulled down almost to the eyes even in the sketch.

Yeah! That's the guy alright. And now I know why I wasn't sure he was the man when I saw him. He has no hat on today but put a hat on him and I can tell you. He's the guy."

Chapter 9

The policemen stood looking over their Search results. " I can see no resemblance here."

Owen was quick to respond. "But, Sergeant, I told you if you'd put his hat on him, it would look the same. Someone should go get his hat and you'll see what I mean. I've watched him several times going in and coming out of the woods. This HAS to be him!"

Constable Andrews spoke quietly to Owen as he nodded toward the door. The two stepped outside and Andrews said, "If you believe that hat will change him into who you think he is, then we're going after that hat to prove it."

"I'm almost certain that's the hat he usually wears. I know the sketch looks nothing like him, but I swear that's him in the hat."

"We'll know shortly," the constable answered. "We'll take it back and put it on him...that should do the trick."

Owen was beginning to have his doubts. "I certainly hope I'm right! This case needs to be solved."

Constable Andrews and Owen went into the house. The door had been left open when the Constable nabbed the stranger, so they walked straight in. Things were a mess, but they could tell he had left the bed in a hurry. Things were strewn about everywhere. As they looked about for his hat, they found it crumpled up in a corner. Owen straightened it out and insisted they leave.

" I don't think so, Owen. This place needs to be gone over with a fine-toothed comb and I'm not leaving till we've done that! You go check the other rooms to see if he has anything in there. We've got to make a full recovery, or this case will go nowhere."

Owen did as he was instructed. With the exception of the bathroom and kitchen, the other rooms were entirely empty. In the bathroom, the stranger had stripped some paper off the walls for his personal use.

In the kitchen, there was very little food to be found...a half-eaten bottle of peanut butter, a small bottle of pickles and some ritz crackers along with about a dozen teabags. There was also a small amount of coffee in a jar and some water in an old teakettle. It was a sad looking state of affairs.

"I'm afraid there's not too much here. A bit of torn wallpaper in the bathroom and barely anything to eat in the kitchen. I wonder how he's been getting by."

The constable was going through garbage he had pulled from under the bed.

"There has to be a bag here somewhere. Someone said he had a bag when he first came. If we could find that, we might get some additional information. You didn't come across a bag anywhere, did you?"

"Uh, uh! No sign of a bag. Did you look everywhere? Behind that old kitchen stove, for instance."

"No, I've been too busy trying to clean up around this bed and underneath it. Did you think to check the closets?"

"No, but I will." Owen opened the first closet door he came to. It was just off the hall between the kitchen and bathroom.

"Ah hah! I do believe we have something here," he said. He pulled a battered bag from the closet.

"May I have it, please? Since you're not a policeman, you wouldn't be authorized to check things. I will look after that."

Owen passed him the bag, which the policeman set on the kitchen table, the only uncluttered spot he could find.

"Now, this should help us! This is a bag that belongs to the place he came from, and if it's a product of the place or if he was a resident there, we should find a name tag in it, or possibly G.G. and the name of the place or institution where he was residing."

He turned the bag to and fro, then practically wrong side out.

"Ah hah! Here we have it." The patch on the bottom of the bag, which he pulled off, was not very clear. It was obvious that it had been around a long time, but the Constable was able to read it.

"It says here, 'A.A. Who loves the sea and has travelled from one sea to another. 'The West Coast Institution For The Mentally Incapacitated'"

"Well, A.A. is sure not Gus Griffin! I guess I must be wrong!" Owen looked at the policeman, who was also trying to fathom this out.

"Well, I'll be!" The constable and Owen set out for the police headquarters, the constable with the bag and Owen with the hat.

Chapter 10

The Constable and Owen took the hat and tag from the bottom of the bag and went back toward town. They were both puzzled as to who they had on their hands, so it gave them a reason to travel deep in thought. Who could this guy be?

They got out of the car, still very pensive and went into the station.

"Let's see that hat!" The Sergeant blared. "If this will make the difference, we'll soon know for sure who this guy is."

He pulled the hat down on the stranger's head, but it fell completely over his eyes. The Sergeant rolled his eyes at Owen.

"Does that look like a FIT to you and NOW do you recognize the stranger?"

Owen looked at the stranger. It DID resemble the man, but

this was not the man he recognized. There had to be another hat back at that place! They must have missed it.

"I'm sure there's a hat that does fit him somewhere in that house! We just must have missed it."

"Look at the guy! Is there any resemblance?"

Owen shook his head. "I really can't say there is a great deal! But the hat does change the picture."

They both realized they were no further than ever. In fact! They were almost back where they started. No amount of reasoning could convince the man to speak, so they were still at a loss.

The Sergeant went back to look up the Search list again. There was nothing new on the sketch that would help them out. It said only that he loved to travel from coast to coast as he loved the Oceans, both Atlantic and Pacific. He had been picked up three times, once on the Atlantic Coast and twice on the Pacific. It appeared that he was seeking something, but it was never clear what he was after. He was not a married man and was very unsettled. Relatives - unknown. He didn't seem to be a thief, but there was an additional note added today. He liked children's playgrounds and could be seen hanging out in parks.

"Well, do we have any reason to hold this man?"

"I think we can let him go back to his place and just keep track of his movements every day. Surely that will give us some clues."

The Sergeant told his captors to let him go. "We'll keep a closer eye on things and make sure of his every move."

Owen was not happy with the choice, but the police seemed to be okay with it, so they let him go. He started limping back down the highway toward his house. They watched him out of sight, then they all got together for a meeting about their next move.

This stranger had no uncertainty about his next move. This HAD to be done and the sooner, the better.

He had made up his mind.

Kim took Astrid outside after her short after-lunch nap.

"Thank goodness! They caught that bad man who sneaks around here." She told Astrid. "Today, mama's going to leave you in your swing for a minute while she calls the police station to see what they will do with him. I hope by this time he is in a cell waiting for trial. Here! Let me give you a good push to get your swing moving."

Kim started the swing moving, then hurried into the house. Dialling the police station, she asked if Owen was there.

"Just a minute, please." She could hear the policeman in the background asking if Owen Boone was around. In a few minutes, her husband came to the phone.

"Sorry, I was just on my way to the car to come home. Is something wrong?"

"Not really. I just wanted to know what they're going to do with that man?"

"Is Astrid with you?"

"Well, no. I left her on the swing a minute so I could call you."

"Quick! Go get her right now! NOW! I'll be home in a few

minutes." He hung up and Kim hurried out to the backyard. The swing was still swaying, but there was no Astrid to be found.

"Oh, God! No!" Kim cried repeatedly as she searched the area. "Please, Lord, let me find her!"

Escaping with the child as quickly as he could, the stranger kept explaining to the fussing child, "Don't cry, sweetie. Papa will take you to a nice place by the Ocean and give you to a nice man. Don't be afraid. You will Iike the nice man."

He went as quickly as possible and took his hat from the back of the door. He snatched up his bag and went out with the baby to the highway. He crossed the road and went into the woods on the opposite side. In minutes he was deep into the woods.

The child was clearly frightened and now crying, so his efforts were to get as far from the village as he could. He knew exactly where he was headed. It may take him over two days, but he would connect with his contact. She cried another hour, then fell asleep. He put her down beneath a low-hanging bough and took some time to look for berries. He approached an open space that had a few low bushes. He checked them out and found a handful of raspberries. Maybe this would make her happy. He wished he had time to get some for himself, but it was necessary to keep the baby quiet. He wondered if this was anywhere near the place he had seen previously with a brook running through it. He had no time to look for the brook. He couldn't take a chance on the child awakening and wandering off.

When he got back, Astrid was still sleeping, so he lay down beside her and soon nodded off. When she awoke, he gave her the raspberries. She was hungry and they didn't quite satisfy her, so she started howling again. Could she be heard from this part of the forest? He was a nervous wreck. He sure didn't want to be found with the child. He knew if he could make it another mile or so, there was an old run-down cabin where they could spend the night. There was nothing to do but put up with her crying and keep moving onward the cabin. It was almost dark when he reached the cabin, and the child was needing a drink. He placed her in what he felt was a safe place and set out for the spring, which he knew was nearby. There was only one problem. He had nothing to get the water with. The only thing he could do was bring the child to the water.

He went back to the cabin but noticed he had left the door open. The child was nowhere in sight.

Chapter 11

The stranger hoped the child would show up on her own. He had no idea where she could have gone, but he checked around the area with no luck. He really didn't want to go too far in case the child wandered back to the cabin. He didn't hear her whimpering or crying as she had been. Where on earth could she be?

He was feeling really hungry himself and had no food with him, so he knew it must be hard on the baby. What would he tell his contact? How could he say he lost the child? What explanation could he give?

He decided to check around the property once again. Surely she couldn't have drowned in the brook. He was afraid she might have gone behind him and lost her way.

It wasn't far to the spring. He would double-check. Anxiously he made his way back down the path. He reached the spring, but she wasn't there. He thought he heard her whimpering somewhere, though. He stopped and listened carefully. Sure enough...that was her. He was quite sure. He walked down along the little brook, but there was no sign of her. Where could she be? He listened again and though he could still hear a faint whimper, it seemed to be coming from further away. Maybe he should walk the other way. He turned and headed upstream. The whimper became a bit louder and as he approached a place where the brook was very shallow...indeed, it was scarcely flowing...he could hear a slight splashing sound. Just ahead of him was a curve in the flow of the little brook and the minute he rounded the curve, he saw her. She was sitting in the brook and her clothes were soaked. Had she fallen in? As he came near, she reached out her arms to him.

The stranger reached to pick her up and he was almost in tears. He didn't realize he felt so strongly about the child. She clung to him and he hugged her close. Should he keep this little one as his own or turn her over to the contact? He had never experienced such a closeness before. This was something new for him, although he often enjoyed watching the kids in the park or at their playground.

He carried her back to the cabin, but she fussed continually. He we sure it was because she was hungry. He himself felt famished, but he had brought nothing with them to eat. He was in too big a hurry when he left with the child.

He put her down to sleep but she fussed for another hour before she fell off to sleep. He didn't blame her. He knew they were both very tired and felt sure a lot of it was due to their lack of food. He was sorry he could offer the little girl nothing. He had no diapers for the baby, but she was smelling a little better after sitting in the brook. He knew there was nothing he could do about it, but he was sure his contact would know what to do. He figured two days would bring him to the contact. Then the stranger would earn some money and be able to buy a meal and continue his walk to the Atlantic Coastline. He loved the sea and could sit on the sand all day, just observing the waves. He could hardly wait!

How would they get through the next few days without something to eat, though? Maybe, when he got through the forest, he would come across a vegetable garden and find a few things to eat. But the baby might not be able to eat raw vegetables. If they could find some cucumbers, he would use his jack knife to peel them and let her eat the centre. Or they might find a ripe tomato in someone's garden. She might be able to eat that like an apple. He could not keep his mind off food, but about an hour after the baby went to sleep, he drifted off with his growling stomach.

Chapter 12

The baby had awakened a couple of times in the night, but he managed to shush her back to sleep with a great deal of effort. It took awhile, and it was mostly a case of her crying herself to sleep again. Each time she awakened, he wondered how he could get her some food, berries or something! But knew he had no solution.

He awoke about 4:30 a.m. to sounds outside the cabin. He lay quietly, hoping the baby wouldn't wake up, but still, the sound of movement and a sniffing sound kept up. What should he do? Dare he look out the one window in the cabin to see where the noise was coming from? He thought it best that he should lie very still and if it was a bear, it would possibly go off after awhile.

Outside, the three policemen followed the police dog to the cabin. Once at the door, it stopped and looked at the following men. They sneaked up to the cabin. One tried to see in the single window, but it was still too dark to see properly. Finally, the Sergeant beckoned to his constables.

"Who wants to burst in? Do I have a volunteer? Be careful he does not hold the child as a shield. Put cuffs on him and lead him out, then one of you get the child and walk back the way we came to the child's home and deliver her to her parents."

"I'll go in!" Constable Andrews stepped up to the door. "Here I go!"

He gave the door a good push and it flew open easily.

The stranger sat up in the bed in alarm, but Constable Andrews immediately caught hold of his wrists and pulled them behind him, clamping the locks on his wrists. Corporal Baye followed him in and picked up the child.

She started crying, but he carried her back the path he had come in, while she cried the whole way. It was a five-mile journey and he was more than happy to arrive at the home of the Boone family.

"Oh, thank God!" Kim cried. "She's home safely!

Oh! Thank you, Officer. We so appreciate your efforts!"

"It's part of my job, Friend. I'm glad I could help. We caught the stranger hiding in a cabin. Now he has to be brought to justice. That may take some time as we still don't know his name, but we will find out. He may refuse to talk but we do have ways and means. I'm just glad I could deliver your daughter to you."

"And so am I! You have a good day, Officer, and tell your detachment we send our thanks."

After the officer left, Astrid continued to cry while her mother got her a bottle of milk. She devoured it voraciously and her mother stripped her down for a bath. She was a different child after getting bathed and fed. When her father came in, she reached her arms up with a big smile and he hugged her to him.

"Thank God, my little girl is home!"

The Sergeant walked the stranger out of the woods and Constable Andrews brought the dog. They gave the dog a treat for his good work at sniffing out the culprit and the baby. The stranger was put in a cell to await his future trial and the Sergeant went back to the books to see what they could learn about the stranger. He still refused to speak to anyone, but the Sergeant pulled up the tag which had been in the bottom of his bag.

"It looks like we might have a problem pinning this kidnapping on the stranger. It would appear that he is mentally incompetent. In fact, I think he may be pretty harmless from what I read on the screen. I still don't think the sketch looks like him, but if we can only get his name, I think we can tie this case up and send him back to the mental facility from which he escaped."

"Constable Andrews, why don't you check on our prisoner and see that all is okay? If he has a mental condition, I think we need to watch him carefully as I'm not sure what he might do to himself."

The Constable went out to check on the stranger. He found him doubled over hanging on to his stomach.

"Having trouble?"

The Constable went back to the desk. He said nothing but shook his head.

"Can I get you something to help?"

Again he failed to speak. After awhile, he made a motion of putting something in his mouth.

"Oh, so you're hungry! Eh?" He nodded his head and the Constable went back to the desk.

"Sergeant, I'm going to duck out a minute on an errand. I'll be right back."

The Sergeant nodded and the Constable dashed out. In a few minutes he was back with a burger, fries and a coke. As he gave it to the stranger, the man actually began to cry. 'Wow,' the Constable thought, 'he really does have mental problems'. He would tell the Sergeant about the strange reactions.

When he went back to check, the stranger had already laid down on the cot and was fast asleep.

He went back to the Sergeant.

"We need to get in touch with that mental institution tomorrow."

The Sergeant nodded his head. "Plan to!"

Chapter 13

"The West Coast Institution for the Mentally Incapacitated," the Sergeant read. "How many times must I call there? Surely someone is available to answer. They can't all be busy, or they don't have a very large staff."

"What answer do you get?" Andrews asked.

"Well, at first, I got no answer, but the last call I made said, 'This number is no longer in service'. I don't know what's going on, whether they're busy or if they've gone out of business."

"There must be some way to find out."

"I'm going to call the province of BC and find out how to get hold of them."

It took most of the day to finally get the information, but the Sergeant finally hung up with a look of total disgust.

"Then I guess that's that!"

"Now, what's the story?"

"They put me through the grind. I just had to call our Police Precinct out there to get any information, aside from the others telling me there was no such place. Their government doesn't keep very good records apparently, or they could have told me that.

"Superintendant Johns informed me the West Coast Institution has been closed for years. It is now located in Burnaby and is called 'The Centre for Mental Health'. He suggested I call them tomorrow and try to track down this guy's records. He also gave me their phone number."

"Has anyone checked on the prisoner today?"

"You can check on him if you like, Constable Andrews. You two seem to have such a strange affinity!"

"I have empathy! But I wouldn't call it affinity."

The constable smiled as he went out. Being from the West Coast and having never known his missing father, Andrews felt a weird attraction to the stranger who seemed so helplessly at loose ends. He wasn't sure why he should feel this way, but he did.

The prisoner sat with his cap pulled down as usual, his back against the wall. He merely peered at Andrews then looked away.

"Well! I see we made it through the night okay.

How are we feeling today! Is everything normal?"

There was no answer. The stranger got up off the floor and moved to his bunk, sitting glumly on the side of it. He stared at the floor.

'This stranger is certainly a 'strange' one!' Andrews thought. He had brought a magazine to give the fellow but forgot it in the car.

"I'll be back in a minute," he said as he went out to the car. In a few minutes, he was back with the 'People' magazine, which he thrust through the bars.

" I brought you something to read! Or at least, to look at."

He extended the magazine through the bars. At first, the stranger just stared at it, then he slowly reached out and accepted it. He glanced at the cover but failed to open it up while Andrews watched. Finally, the constable left him alone and walked back to the Sergeant.

He paused for a minute in front of his boss. "I know this sounds strange to you, but I can't help but feel a sense of compassion for that strange man. In a rather weird way! I think he was really fond of that little girl he captured, and I believe he almost thought she was his."

"Well, I've heard a lot of weird theories in my life, but this beats them all! Have you lost your mind? That man kidnapped the child...no two ways about it! Call it what you will in the eyes of the law; he is a criminal."

"I guess you're right! But I can't shake this feeling of compassionate empathy!

"Go home and get a good night's rest and you may come to your senses. Good night, Andrews! You're off for the rest of the day. We'll be leaving in another hour anyway. See you in two days since tomorrow is your day off."

Chapter 14

After catching up with most of his morning chores, the Superintendant decided to call 'The Centre for Mental health' located in Burnaby. He dialed the number Superintendant Johns had given him and someone came on the line.

"Good Morning. This is Sergeant Sparks from the Police Department in Clements, New Brunswick, and I require some information on a former patient of the West Coast Institution for the Mentally Incapacitated.

We are holding him as a prisoner here and he refuses to answer our questions. Can you provide any further information?"

"First, we will need his name."

"I'm sorry. We don't know his name. He won't tell us and we found he has very little information on him."

"I doubt we'll be able to help and I'm afraid there's not

much we can do! But fill me in on what you have now and I'll try to locate his original file from the West Coast Institution. But you realize, do you not, that their records will go back many years. We took members of that Institution in over 30 years ago, so records go back a long way."

"Well, all I can tell you, Sir, is what we got from his records while he was in there. I'm sure there will be more records on him, but this gives us a clue. We searched the bag he carries and found the name of the West Coast Institute and the initials A.A. They also said he especially likes children, so we figured we had a pedophile on our hands. I do think we've been proven wrong as he kidnapped a child and felt it was his own. He used her very well, so maybe he just has a love for children."

"Well, Sir. I'll check what I can find from the West Coast Institute under those initials, but I really can't promise anything right now."

"I hope you can come up with something!"

"It sounds pretty hopeless, but we'll try. If we find anything, we'll give you a call."

"Thank you, Sir! I hope you can come up with something."

The Sergeant hung up with a feeling of despair. It seemed almost hopeless. How could anything be accomplished without the stranger's name?

He was still contemplating the situation when the phone rang.

"Sergeant Sparks here."

"Hello, Sergeant! I think we have an emergency on our

hands. We've just had the stranger locked up for a week, but I think his contact may be here looking for him. Oh, I forgot to say, this is Owen Boone and we have Astrid inside with us but there is a man sneaking around the stranger's house. I think it may be his contact. He started up our driveway a while ago, but I walked down and talked to him in the driveway, hoping he would come no further. He wanted to know the name of the man next door, so I told him I didn't know.

"At least he's smart enough for that," the man said.

"When I asked what he meant, he answered, 'nothing in particular'. Maybe you should come and check this guy out."

"I'll be there in a sec!"

The Sergeant took Constable Byrd with him and drove out to the old house. The door of the house was open and the policemen sneaked up to take a look. The man was looking through the cupboards, obviously looking for something to eat.

"Hands up!" The Sergeant exclaimed, stepping into the house with his gun drawn. The man turned and put his hands in the air. Constable Byrd grabbed his hands and put on handcuffs, then led him toward the door.

"What's going on here. I'm just here visiting my friend."

"Yes, we'll see to that! We're taking you to see him now." The Sergeant chuckled as he led the man to his police car.

Chapter 15

The next week passed without any word from BC. The Sergeant was not happy with the process as they had two prisoners on their hands and very little information on them. He waited but rather impatiently. The wheels of the law turn slowly, but at last, the NB Police Precinct got a call.

"Good morning, Sergeant Sparks. I'm calling from BC about the prisoners you are holding...well, I guess I should say the ' prisoner'. One is truly a criminal, but the other is simply a deluded mental patient. We have all the details on the criminal. His name is Alfred Snow and we have been trying for years to capture him. He is a well-known pedophile who picks up children and sells them to very unsavoury people or keeps them for his own satisfaction. Our Crime Unit has been trying to keep track of him for years, but he keeps on the move, going from Coast to Coast. He has been captured once before, but he got away. He needs to be in prison and we will send a unit to bring him back as soon as possible. He comes from Victoria, BC., and is to be tried there, commencing with his first crime. The sooner we can get hold of him, the better."

"You are more than welcome to him anytime!"

"We will send out a unit to get him right away. As to the other fellow, we searched his record from the West Coast Institution and found that he was admitted as a young man of 25 and found to be very delusional. Unlike the other character, he was once a married man, but, so far, there is no report of any family. His wife had him committed, but there is no record of her following up on his condition. It seems rather sad, really, as it appears that somehow this Alfred got his hands on him and convinced him to 'go into business with him'. He was weak-minded enough to believe it was a legitimate business deal, so he agreed. He has been in and out of the mental institution several times. At times, he was released and at other times, this Alfred character helped him escape. He has not been recaptured since his last escape from the West Coast Institution a number of years ago. I think he was more or less considered a lost cause. But it would appear he has travelled from West to East and back again several times. He loves the Sea and can sit harmlessly by it for hours but is often on a search for a child to bring back to his contact, Snow. If we can find out anything else, we will let you know, but he seems pretty harmless and I almost think you could let him go."

"Thanks, Officer! Perhaps we'll do that, but I think we'll try to get a little more information first. I appreciate what you've passed along to us, though. We'll get the 'real' prisoner ready for your arrival in the meantime."

It was only after he hung up that Sergeant Sparks realized he hadn't gotten the mental patient's name yet.

Owen and Kim were keeping a close watch on their little girl, always keeping her in sight. She was quickly picking up English words now, and every day she wanted to go out to play. If Owen was at work, Kim would take her out, but when Owen was home, she became 'Daddy's girl' and only he could make her happy. Today was one of those days. Owen was letting her go down the slide when Constable Byrd drove in.

"Well, hello to you!"

Constable Byrd tipped his hat in reply.

"It's good to see you again, Owen. Have you been keeping busy?"

"You bet I have. If I'm not at work, you will find me here in the backyard with my daughter. She won't let me out of her sight!"

"Well, I have a task you might prefer not to do, but we need to run a final test before we can let one of our prisoners go, so we're asking if you will cooperate."

"I guess that will depend on the test," Owen answered.

"Then I might as well tell you right off...it will take a lot of trust on your part, but we will be watching all the time. We would like you to bring Astrid down to the stranger's cell and see how he reacts. We want to know if he just likes children or if he is a pedophile.

It's very important as we're thinking of letting him go."

"Do you realize what you're asking? That would be almost impossible. I know Kim would never allow it!"

"Well, we think he's pretty harmless, but we need to make sure. Why don't we go talk to Kim and see how she feels?"

"You can try, but I don't think you'll get anywhere. She doesn't want to expose Astrid to that stranger any more than I do."

Owen picked up the little girl and the policeman went in behind them.

Chapter 16

"Good morning, Kim!" The policeman greeted her.

"And the same to you, Sir." Kim was all smiles.

"I'm not sure you'll see me as a 'nice' man when I deliver my message. As you know, the stranger is in a jail cell, being held for child kidnapping, but it would appear he is really not guilty of such an offence. Please understand me - I know he took your child, but he is mentally incompetent and I'm sure he was really not aware of what he was doing. His contact had told him he was helping to 'rescue' children who would be given back to their real parents. This was totally untrue, but the stranger, being mentally challenged, did not understand that. He really believed he was helping children get 'home'.

We truly think he is an innocent victim of circumstances and would like to prove that he has a genuine love for children. This is where the hard part comes in. We would like to take Astrid to see the man in his jail cell. We will be in another spot but will constantly watch for reactions. If she acts fearful or does not want to see him, we will be nearby and immediately rescue her. You may both come into our observation room and watch the proceedings. Do you think you could manage to let us do this?"

Kim looked at the man in disbelief!

"Are you crazy? Do you realize what you are saying? How could you ask such a thing?"

The constable put up his hand. "Just a minute. You may think I am crazy, but the truth is, this poor man seems to have lived under a delusion all his life. He has worked with a contact who told him the children he had brought would be returned to their 'real' parents. Meanwhile, the stranger appears to have loved children and would not harm them. He wanted so badly to have a child to love, and yet it seems, life had passed him by. For this poor, mentally challenged man to be locked away for the rest of his life seems so unfair.

"I promise you," the constable added, "Astrid will not be harmed. We will make sure of that and you can be there to observe and intervene if necessary. But I am sure it will not go that far. We will WATCH the two of them all the while."

Kim groaned. "How can you ask this of us?"

"I'll give you time to think about it, but we hope you will consent."

"This requires more than thought," Owen added. "This is a matter of prayer."

"Then I shall leave you two to think and pray. I will call you later. Good day to you."

With that, the policeman donned his cap and left.

"Come on, Kim. It's time to pray."

Owen clasped hands with his wife and they wept their way through their agony. By the time they finished praying, he hoped Kim felt the way he did.

"Honey, have you heard from the Lord? I was so disgusted with the stranger's actions that I'm afraid I had an unforgiving spirit. But in addition to our child, there is another life involved here. What do you think?"

"Oh, Owen! I'm leaving everything up to your decision. You make the choice and I'll back you up, whatever you decide."

"Then get her ready and I'll call the Police Department."

He dialled the number and waited a few minutes before Constable Andrews came to the phone.

"Hello again, Sir. This is Owen Boone and we've made a decision."

"Which is?"

"We'll be in with the baby right away."

"I'm sure you won't regret it!"

As soon as he saw Kim come downstairs with Astrid, a huge lump filled his throat. What was he doing to his own baby girl?

They followed him out to the car, got in, and Owen said, "Let's wait a minute right here, Kim. We're going to lay hands on this baby and pray for her protection."

When they finished praying, Owen started the car and went toward the Police Station. Without a word, they got out and Owen carried her inside. She had become familiar with the Sergeant's face and allowed him to take her to the prisoner's cell. Owen and Kim popped into the observation room with Constable Andrews, where they took up an observation post.

They saw the Sergeant going toward the cell. The stranger was sitting on the side of his bunk, but his face lit up and he stood at the sight of the child.

Chapter 17

The minute Astrid saw the stranger, the light of recognition filled her face and she reached out her arms to him. The Sergeant opened the cell door and passed him the child, then joined the group on the observation deck. They watched quietly as the stranger held her, then, for the first time ever, they heard him speak.

"Papa's so happy they brought you back to him! Where have you been, baby? Papa missed you so much!" He gave the child a hug and kissed her forehead. "Do you think they will let me keep you now? I missed the date with my contact, so I have no money, but we will get by somehow." The child reached up and tugged at his beard.

"Oh, I know, I know. It needs to come off, and it will someday when we get back to the big house where Papa lives.

I hope that is soon. I sure wish we had a swing in here. Papa would give you a big push!"

The Sergeant stepped outside and the Constable joined him as they went the short distance to the cell.

"Time to go, baby," the Sergeant said as he reached for the child, but she held on to the man's neck. With tears running down his wrinkled face and dripping into his mangled beard, he pulled her off and passed her to the Sergeant, who stepped outside and gave her to her parents.

They left the building with tears in their own eyes.

"How could we have been so judgemental?" Owen asked.

"But we had lost our child and how were we to know what was going on?" Kim wiped at the tears on her cheeks.

Back at the Police Station, Constable Andrews and the Sergeant brought the Stranger back to the office for questioning. He sat bolt upright with a look of near-terror on his face. What would happen to him now? Would he be sent off to prison today? Why did they take his little girl away?

The Constable started the questioning.

"We watched you with the child and we know you can speak, so first, would you like to tell us your name?"

The man didn't answer.

"Let's not make this difficult. Where are you from, or where is your home?"

The man stuttered, but he finally got it out.

"BBBritish Columbia."

"What town in British Columbia?"

"Langley BC."

"Do you have a home there?"

"I was living in an apartment till my woman kicked me out."

The Sergeant was taking it all in. 'Boy, do we have this guy on a roll,' he thought.

"How many children did you have?"

"One," The stranger answered, "but I don't know where my own child is!" A tear slipped down his cheek. "I wish my contact would find the baby for me."

"Well, I'm sure the baby would be a grown-up now. How many years since you were kicked out by your woman?"

"I don't remember, but it was a long time ago."

"Are you ready to tell us your name?"

No answer.

"When we learn your name, we will let you go, but you had better give it some thought because we can not let you go until we know who you are. Then we can investigate you properly. For now, we'll take you back to your cell and give you a chance to think about this."

They led the stranger back to his cell, where he sat and thought about anything he could remember. If they let him go, should he go back to Langley to look for his child, or should he go on his way to the Atlantic Coast? He would love to go sit in the sand by the sea for awhile. Maybe that's where he would go.

Chapter 18

"Do you think he will come back to the ramshackle old house if they release him? " Kim's voice held a hint of fear.

"I'm not sure, but I suppose it's the only place he can come to. I only hope they make him understand he is not to 'take' children. That may take a bit of effort."

"I just thought of something that might help."

"And what was that, my dear?"

"Well, if he moves back in next door...it's a frightening thought, but it might work...maybe we could let him come over awhile in the afternoon to play with Astrid. We would both be there to see that all goes well."

"My dear wife, I think you might be jumping the gun! Don't you understand that he will still think she is his child? What if he tries to escape with her again?"

"I don't think that will happen. I'm sure they'll get through to him why he cannot do that. Trust me and see what happens."

"You sound much more confident than I feel, but we'll wait and see."

The stranger sat in his cell, waiting for his captors to take him for questioning again. Should he tell them his name? Did they have a lot of information on him? And would they use it against him if he told them who he was? His whole world could crumble against him if they knew he had escaped from that awful Institution in the West years ago. Would they send him back there if they knew his name? No! It was best that he keep it to himself. Then he wouldn't be put in that place again! The only reason he had ever been in there was his woman's fault. She had signed him in there and then she disappeared with the baby...his baby! How cruel could she get?

As he pondered what to do, the cell door was opened and the Sergeant led him to the interrogation room. Constable Andrews had again been left to do the questioning.

"Good morning, Friend," he began. "We have left you to yourself for three days, hoping you would choose to tell us your name. Are you ready to do that?"

Again the man did not speak.

"I hope you understand all the things you can be charged with if you do not tell us your name."

"I...I haven't done anything wrong."

"What have you been working at?"

"Delivery."

"What kind of delivery?"

"I was told not to say."

"You may not realize it, but you need to tell me for your own good. Now, WHAT were you delivering?"

"I was helping get babies back to their parents."

"I don't think so! Did you have a contact?"

"Yes, of course. I gave them to my contact and he gave them back to their parents."

"That's what you thought, but we caught your buddy and we're sending him off to prison. You were kidnapping children for him. Did you realize that?"

"Oh, no! Never! He was getting them back to their families."

"I hate to disillusion you, but that was really not the case. So you see, you have kidnapped a good number of babies. How do you feel about that?"

"If that is true, then I am horrified! I can't believe I would do such a thing!"

"Well, it is true! And I think you need to give us your name so we can get this cleared up."

"But I cannot do that! You must never find out my name, or I'll be sent back to that awful place in the West. No, I can't tell my name and I hope you never learn who I am."

As usual, they took him back to his cell to consider the matter.

Chapter 19

Astrid sat in her high chair, having a snack. She munched on her crackers and went over a lot of gibberish while she snacked.

Owen was late coming home for lunch, so Kim joined Astrid at the table. She had prepared a fish chowder and was really enjoying it when the child began asking about her father.

"Dada? Dada?"

"Dada is still at work."

"Mama? Mama?" The child continued.

"Why Mama is right here," Kim said, pointing to herself.

"Papa? Papa?" The child continued.

Kim was completely taken aback. Why would she say, Papa? She wondered, and who was Papa? Then she recalled how the little girl had called the stranger Papa. Surely she wasn't wanting him to show up!

The door opened and in walked Dada. The little girl's arms automatically reached out to him.

"Dada!" She said as he picked her up from her high chair.

He kissed his wife and gave her the child until he washed his hands, then sat down at the table. Kim placed the baby back in the high chair and dipped some chowder into her husband's bowl. He bowed his head and gave thanks. Kim waited until he had started eating, then told him about Astrid's strange requests.

Owen chuckled, then added, "Surely she's not missing that smelly stranger."

"I don't know how else to describe it unless she just thought of him and came up with the name."

"Children can be indecipherable sometimes!"

"I'll say! Would you like some more chowder?"

"Don't mind if I do."

Kim refilled his bowl and as she did, Astrid said, "Chow-chow?"

"Now, what is she asking for?" Kim couldn't interpret her request.

"She wants chowder, of course. Say 'Chow-der' Astrid. 'Chow-der'." But the child only smiled. Owen gave her a taste of his chowder and she licked her lips in satisfaction.

"She's ready for regular food. We should be giving her more of it...just make sure pieces are small and there are no bones in it."

"She's been eating regular foods for quite a while now. After all, she's nearly two. It's just that I haven't given her fish chowder before. Now that I know she likes it, I'll give her some next time."

Kim got a washcloth and washed Astrid's face and hands.

"Now for a little nap, and then we'll go outside." She took Astrid upstairs for her nap.

When she came down, Owen said, "I guess they're having trouble getting the stranger to tell them his name. He seems to be afraid they'll send him back out West to the mental institution. I can't imagine what they did to him there to frighten him so much of the place."

"We never know what goes on behind closed doors in some places."

Meanwhile, the stranger was back for more interrogation.

"Do you think you might be ready to tell us your name?"

The stranger merely stared at the floor.

"You'll be able to go see that little girl again who calls you 'Papa'. Would you like that?"

The stranger's eyes filled with tears, but he beamed proudly.

"Did you say she is not my child?"

"I did! She is your neighbour's child, but she loves you like a Papa. I think you might be able to visit her when you go back to your house, that is, if her parents let you. You almost sold their child, so they may be quite angry. But they are good Christian people, so they might forgive you. But the only way we'll ever know is if you'll tell us your name."

"I dare not do that. I might be sent back out to the crazy house."

"I doubt it. But let's change the subject. Have you ever been to church?

"Never!"

"Then I have an idea." He glanced at the Sergeant, who nodded his head and the Constable continued, "Why don't you come with me this weekend to church?"

"I...I...wouldn't know what to wear or what to do."

The Constable turned to the Sergeant.

"Do you suppose he could spend the weekend with me? I promise to watch him like a hawk."

"Well..he is a prisoner...I'm not sure...oh, go ahead! As long as you watch him continually and bring him back on Monday to his cell!"

"I promise! He won't get out of my sight!"

"And I'll be certain to stay with you!" The stranger added. "Are there children there?"

"Yes, but you also must promise to stay away from the children."

"Okay, I'll do my very best."

Chapter 20

The first thing Constable Andrews did was run a hot shower for his prisoner guest, then he gave him a razor and told him to neaten up his beard. After that, the Constable gave him a haircut and found him some clean prison clothes. He felt almost certain that the Boone family would never recognize him.

The Constable then took him down the road to visit Ned. When he explained why they were there, Ned was more than happy to help. He quickly dug out an old pair of dress pants and a matching vest but had no white shirt to fit him. Finally, he came out with a beige shirt from former days. The Stranger tried it on and it fit much better. The stranger's old shoes would have to do. They were ready for church. Andrews thanked Ned and took the stranger home again.

"You know, it seems very strange calling you stranger all the time. I wish I knew your name."

There was no answer from the stranger.

Sunday morning - the Lord's day, they got up and the Constable's housekeeper filled them with waffles and coffee. His guest looked a bit uncomfortable, but he certainly enjoyed the food.

As they made their way into the church, they met Owen Boone, who was going downstairs to teach a class, but the Constable stayed close to his guest.

The Minister brought forth a profound message and the Constable could see that the stranger was not looking around but seemed absorbed in the message.

When the Reverend finished his sermon, he asked if there was anyone present who needed the Lord's help. Everyone was asked to bow their heads and close their eyes. Anyone who didn't know the Lord was asked to say after him, "Lord Jesus, forgive my past and walk with me from this day on. Help me to be like you and give me the strength to live for you. In your name. Amen."

He then opened the altar for anyone who would like to come and pray. The Constable went up, taking his guest with him. The stranger bowed his head and was crying his eyes out. "Oh, God, forgive me and make me a new person."

Constable Andrews was overjoyed to hear the man pray for himself. As they left the church, the stranger told the policeman, "It's like a new day has dawned for me. Everything seems new and fresh. Why did I not go to church before?"

"Maybe you weren't invited."

"I never was! Could we go back to my cell this afternoon? I want to tell the Sergeant about it."

"We'll go back as soon as we have dinner."

"I'll tell him my name too!"

"That's wonderful! We're all waiting to hear it."

They finished dinner, the stranger thanked the constable for his kindness and they went on their way.

The Sergeant was home enjoying his weekend, but when he heard the stranger was ready to talk, he made his way into the office.

They all ended up arriving about the same time and the stranger accompanied them into the interrogation room.

"Do you want to do the favours? Sergeant Sparks asked Constable Andrews.

"Why not? I've been doing it right along."

As the stranger took his seat, the constable asked the familiar question.

"And what is your name? We do know that your initials are A.A., but what does that stand for?"

"I know you are from Langley, BC, as am I. Did you ever know an Allison Andrews?"

"No, but I did know an Al Andrews. My mother spoke of him occasionally. I always figured his first name was Allan."

"How would your mother know to call him that?"

"He was her husband, but he left when I was just a baby."

"And what was your mother's name?" The stranger turned pale as he listened to the answer.

"My mother's name was Victoria."

"And what were your siblings named?"

"I have no siblings. My mother worked and paid my way to the Police Academy. I always appreciated that. I just wish my father had still been around to help."

"Well, my name is Allison Andrews and I do believe I've found my missing child, my son, Frederick Andrews. It wasn't my fault that I was not around. That was your mother's fault. She kicked me out and oh, how I missed that beautiful child!"

"But according to your records, you and mother had a girl!"

"Records can be screwed up, Son. Come and give your old dad a hug."

Constable Andrews, with tears, slowly coming to his eyes, grasped the Stranger in a bear hug.

The Sergeant suggested they should release the stranger.

"First," Al Andrews said, "I have something to share with you, Sergeant. Do you go to church?"

"Well, I'm not against the church, but I can't say I go very often."

"Well, you really need to go. It can change your life, as it did mine."

"I'm pleased to hear that, but I can't help wondering why you were in the West Coast Institute."

"My wife put me in there, but I must forgive her now. Otherwise, I wouldn't be here to hear the good news of salvation. I am a changed man!"

"Come on, Father. I'm going to be staying at your house

awhile." Constable Fred Andrews took the stranger's arm. "Let's go!"

THE END